WALKING TO SCHOOL

Poem by
ETHEL TURNER

Pictures by
PETER GOULDTHORPE

ORCHARD BOOKS   *A Division of Franklin Watts, Inc.   New York*

For Adrian

Orchard Books, A division of Franklin Watts, Inc., 387 Park Avenue South, New York, NY 10016
Orchard Books Canada, 20 Torbay Road, Markham, Ontario 23P 1G6

First published in Australia by William Collins Pty Ltd, in association with Anne Ingram Books
Manufactured in the United States of America. Book design by Mina Greenstein.
The text of this book is set in 18 pt. Galliard.
The illustrations are black crayon and watercolor which were camera separated and printed in four colors.
10 9 8 7 6 5 4 3 2 1

Library of Congress Cataloging-in-Publication Data
Turner, Ethel M. Walking to school: poem / by Ethel Turner; illustrated by Peter Gouldthorpe.–1st American ed.   p.   cm.
Summary: Relates, in verse, a little boy's efforts to be brave as he walks alone to school for the first time.
ISBN 0-531-05799-2   ISBN 0-531-08399-3 (lib. bdg.)   [1. Growth–Fiction.   2. Walking–Fiction.   3. Stories in rhyme.]
I. Gouldthorpe, Peter, ill.   II. Title. PZ8.3.T84Wal   1988   [E]–dc19   88-22365   CIP   AC

Now I am five, my father says
  (And what he says you've got to mind)
That mother's not to hold my hand,
  Or even follow me behind,

To see I'm safe. But down the road,
  And all the way up the next street,
I am to walk now quite alone,
  No matter what the things I meet.

Though horrid horses rear and plunge,

And cows come trampling, big and bold,

And fighting boys are strutting out,
I shall have no one's hand to hold.

Still five is really very old;
    It's pretty close to being a man.
Since I a soldier wish to be,
    I s'pose it's time that I began.

I'll swell my chest right out, like this,
   And swing my books behind, just so,
And wear my hat stuck sideways on,
   And whistle all the way I go.

There is a little boy I pass,
   He's always swinging on the gate,
He'll think that I am very old—
   Perhaps he'll think I'm seven, or eight.

There is a little girl I see,
  She's always standing at her door,
When I come whistling boldly past,
  She'll wish that she were more than four.

What I mind most of all are dogs.
   My sister says dogs seldom bite,
But how can I be sure of this!
   Your sisters are not always right.

There is an awful dog I hear;
    It barks and barks as I go by.
I know some day it will get loose,
    And fiercely at my throat will fly.

And other dogs come round and sniff
(I've sandals and my legs are bare).
Perhaps it's true they will not bite;
Perhaps someday I shall not care.

When you were five and walked to school,
    And you met things to tremble at,
Were you as brave as great big men,
    Or did your heart go pit-a-pat?